Ricky's
Big Idea

Martyn Hobbs

HELBLING LANGUAGES

www.helblinglanguages.com

Ricky's Big Idea
by Martyn Hobbs

First published 2011

ISBN 978-3-85272-335-8

Series editor Maria Cleary
Activities by Martyn Hobbs
Illustrated by Lorenzo Sabbatini
Design and layout by Pixarte
Printed by Athesia

About this Book

For the Student

🎧 Listen to the story and do some activities on your Audio CD

Talk about the story

beat• When you see the blue dot you can check the word in the glossary on pages 62-64

For the Teacher

Go to our Readers Resource site for information on using readers and downloadable Resource Sheets, photocopiable Worksheets, Answer Keys and Tapescripts. Plus the full version of the story on MP3.

www.helblingreaders.com

For lots of great ideas on using Graded Readers consult Reading Matters, the Teacher's Guide to using Helbling Readers.

Level 2 Structures

Past simple of *be*	Comparative
Past simple	Comparative with *as...as*
Past simple (common irregular verbs)	Superlative
Be going to	*To* for purpose
Past continuous	Adverbs of manner
Past simple v. past continuous	
	A lot of, not much, not many
Past simple in questions	*And, so, but, because*
Have to / must	Possessive pronouns
Mustn't	

Structures from lower levels are also included.

Contents

Hello, I'm Ricky
and this is my story.
What is my big idea?
Look through the book
and find out!

Before Reading

1 Look at the picture and answer the questions on pages 8 and 9.

The Film Set

Before Reading

1 **Find these things in the picture on page 6 and label them.**

a) keyboard	b) mouse	c) screen
d) video camera	e) monitor	f) key

2 **Find these things in the picture on page 7 and label them.**

a) the set	b) costumes	c) screenplay
d) actor	e) director	f) the lighting

3 **Talk about the pictures on pages 6 and 7. What do you think?**

- Where are the people in the pictures?
- What are they doing?
- What is Ricky looking at on the screen? Why?
- What is happening in the picture on page 7?

4 **The things in the two pictures are important to the story. Why are they important? Can you guess? In groups write a scenario. Include all the things from exercises 1 and 2 in your scenario. Then tell the class. Choose the best scenario.**

5 Listen and write the numbers.

a) 

b) 

c) 

d) 

6 Now answer the questions.

a) Why is Ricky's sister Sonia unhappy?

b) Why is Ricky's father confused?

c) Who is Jack angry with?

d) Who is Jade sending the text message to?

7 Look through the pictures in the book and guess.

- What is Ricky's "big idea"?
- How does he upset his friends and family?

Big ideas can come from very small things.

Early one morning, Archimedes got out of bed and walked into his bathroom. He was remembering all the things he had to do that day – buy food for his cats, tidy the house, do some experiments. He didn't notice that the bath was very full. So he got into it and the hot water poured• onto the floor. He looked at the water for a moment. Then suddenly he jumped out of the bath and shouted: 'Eureka•! Eureka!' Archimedes didn't jump out because the water was hot. He jumped out because he suddenly understood something very important. He understood why some things float• and others sink•. Just think of huge steel ships that weigh millions of kilos. They can float on the sea but a small stone sinks. And Archimedes knew why.

Isaac Newton was sitting in his mother's garden under an apple tree. It was a beautiful day. The birds were singing on the branches and the apples were bright red in the sun. Isaac was thinking (he liked thinking) and enjoying the sunshine, when an apple fell and hit him on the head.

Ouch!

His mother called out from the kitchen: 'Isaac, you are a very silly young man. Don't sit under apple trees!' But Isaac was smiling. He was thinking something very different. He suddenly understood why the Moon moved around the Earth and the Earth moved around the Sun and why the stars stayed in the sky. In fact, he understood how gravity• worked.

Einstein was clever. Very clever. When Einstein was sixteen, he was looking in a mirror at his reflection and he had a strange idea. He thought about a boy sitting on a beam• of light. And that beam of light was travelling across the universe. Einstein thought and thought about this boy and the beam of light and he finally developed his Theory of Relativity. Now that theory is far too difficult to explain here. Even Ricky didn't understand it, and Ricky was probably the cleverest boy in his school. But, like Archimedes and Newton, Einstein proved that big ideas can come from small things.

And Ricky had a big idea.

It all started on a quiet Saturday at home. A very quiet Saturday.

Ricky's sister Jade was in her room.
Ricky's other sister Sonia was in the bathroom.
Ricky's parents were working in their shop. He always helped them with small jobs on Saturday mornings. And everyone agreed that Ricky was a good son.
His friends always asked him for help with their maths and science homework. He did that every Friday evening. And everyone agreed that Ricky was a good friend.
But now it was twelve o'clock and Ricky was free for the rest of the day. So he was doing what he loved doing best. He was sitting on the sofa doing calculations in his head•.

For example, what do you get when you multiply 547 by 125? Or what is 7,904 divided by 16?
He solved the problems, then checked• them with the calculator on his mobile phone. The answers were 68,375 and 494. And Ricky got them right•. And this was Ricky's idea of fun!

He was adding 6,783,209 to 7,534,487 when he heard a terrible scream•. It sounded like Sonia. Then he heard a door open and another scream. That sounded like Jade. Now Ricky liked doing calculations in his head. But this sounded more interesting! He jumped up off the sofa and ran upstairs.

547
494
π
√16

Ricky couldn't believe his eyes.
4
What's going on?
You can see what's going on! Look at my hair! It's a disaster!
He thought quickly. He took out his mobile phone and turned on the video camera.
Calm down, Sonia. How did this happen?
I used a new hair dye.• It's meant to look like this.
What can I do? I'm meeting my new boyfriend this afternoon. He loves my hair. What's he going to say?
There's only one thing you can do. Wash your hair again. Now!

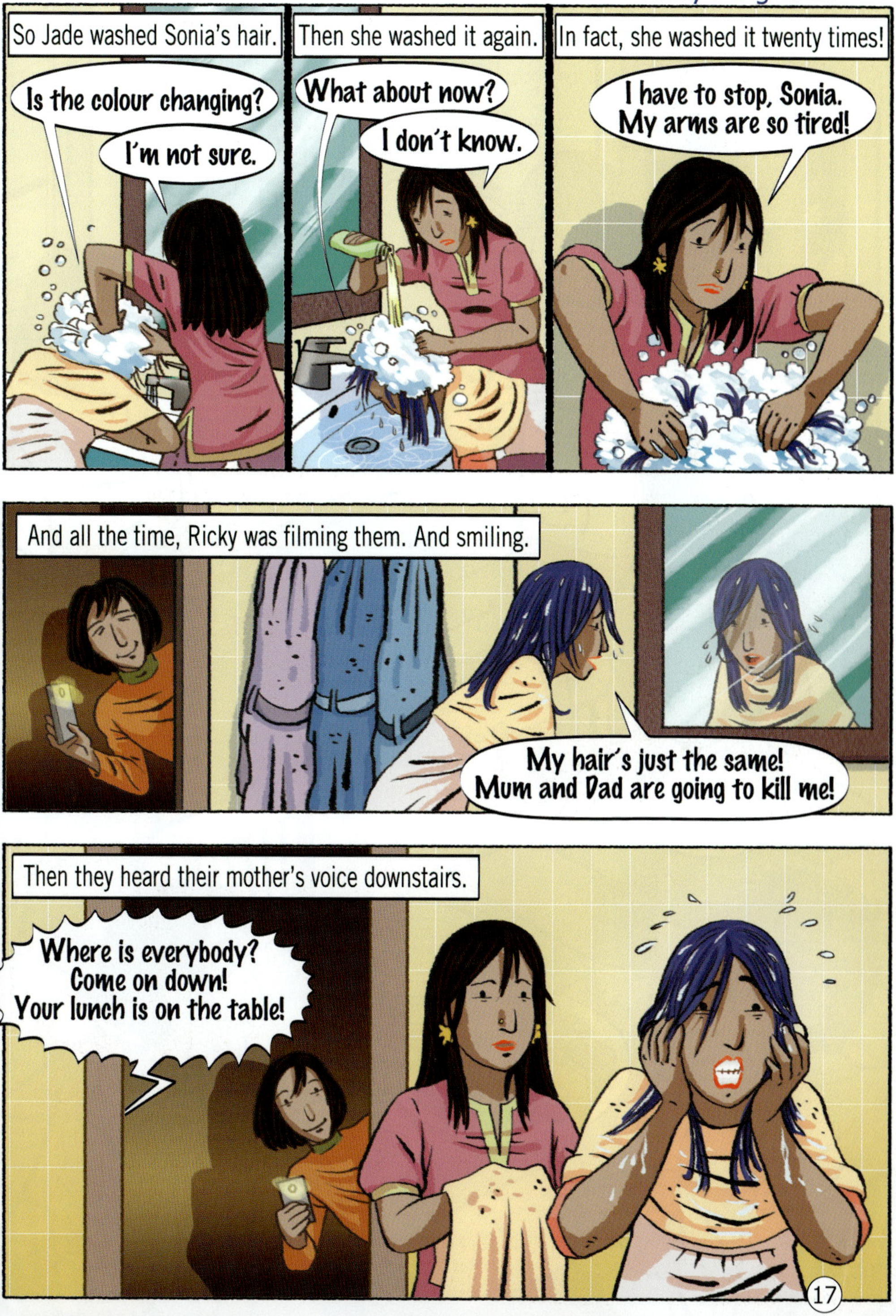
So Jade washed Sonia's hair.
Is the colour changing?
I'm not sure.
Then she washed it again.
What about now?
I don't know.
In fact, she washed it twenty times!
I have to stop, Sonia. My arms are so tired!
And all the time, Ricky was filming them. And smiling.
My hair's just the same! Mum and Dad are going to kill me!
Then they heard their mother's voice downstairs.
Where is everybody? Come on down! Your lunch is on the table!

REC

5 Ricky went down to the kitchen first.

His mother was preparing a salad. His father was trying to do the crossword• in the local paper. It was the easiest crossword in the world but Ricky's dad always found it difficult!

Ricky said 'hi' and sat down. He wanted to be ready for when his sisters arrived.

'Where are those girls?' asked his mother, putting the salad on the table. And then she saw them at the door. Sonia was standing in front of Jade.

'Come on, sit down.'

Jade pushed Sonia towards the table.

'Mum,' she started to say. 'I'm so sorry but...'

And then she fell silent.

Her parents didn't know what to say. They were a bit angry with Sonia. But she looked so silly with her wet blue hair.

'You look like a funny superhero,' said her father.

And they started laughing. They laughed and laughed and couldn't stop. And Sonia thought that was somehow• worse.

And all the time, Ricky was sitting quietly at the kitchen table, secretly filming them on his mobile phone.

That evening, Ricky turned on his computer and got to work. But it wasn't homework. He was doing something very different.

The next morning, Ricky was waiting at the school gates when David and Jack arrived.

'Is everything OK?' David asked.

'Yeah, fine,' said Ricky. 'I just wanted to show you something.'

Jack didn't look interested. After all, Ricky thought science and maths were interesting, and they were so boring!

But Ricky got out his mobile phone and showed them a short film. It was his film of Sonia's hair disaster.

'Oh, wow! That is so funny!' said Jack.

'I didn't have enough footage, really,' explained Ricky. 'But I edited it all together. And then I added music.'

'Did your sisters mind you filming them? asked David.

'They didn't know I was doing it,' said Ricky.

'Well, I think this is just amazing!' said Jack. He never knew Ricky could be so... normal!'

Ricky was very quiet during the day. In fact, he didn't pay much attention to his teachers and the things they were saying. He was thinking about his video of Sonia and her hair and all the things he *didn't* film.

He didn't film the moment when Sonia put the dye on her hair.

He didn't film the look• on her face when she discovered it was bright blue.

And he didn't film the look on Jade's face when she first saw Sonia.

It was a real pain• that he missed that action. He knew his film was funny, but it wasn't funny enough. He just didn't have all the right footage•!

But while his history teacher was talking about Napoleon and the Battle of Waterloo, Ricky had an idea. A big idea.

He could film his family every single moment of the day.

Then he could edit all his footage together.

And finally he could show them the whole film when it was ready.

He could make his own reality TV programme!

Ricky always saved his pocket money, his birthday money and the extra money he got from helping in his parents' shop. So he had enough savings to make his film-making dream a reality.

Ricky went to his favourite computer shop on Westbourne High Street. All the shop assistants wore black clothes and they were crazy about computers and solving technical problems – in fact, all the things that Ricky loved and Jack found stupid! Ricky explained what he wanted to Max and Max found it all. He also gave Ricky lots of useful advice for free.

Ricky made sure nobody was looking when he got home. He took his shopping bag upstairs and hid it at the bottom of his wardrobe.

Then he waited for night to come and for everybody to go to bed.

Ricky lay in his bed and tried not to fall asleep. But finally everybody went to bed and the house was still and quiet. The only noise came from his parents' bedroom. He could hear his father snoring• – and that was a good sign! Ricky looked at his clock. Its bright shining numbers said 02:31. It was time for action! So Ricky switched on his torch, took the bag from the wardrobe and crept• quietly downstairs. He had to be as quiet as a thief•!

Ricky closed the sitting room door then took six small cameras out of the bag. He checked that they all worked. Then he put one on top of the cupboard, one on a picture frame (nobody ever looked at the pictures) and one in the corner. Then he put two cameras in the kitchen and the last one in the hall, pointing at the front door.

After that he went back and looked round the rooms. You couldn't see the cameras. Everything was ready.

Ricky crept quietly up the stairs. He stopped for a moment on the landing•. Everybody was still sleeping. That was good. Then he went back into his room and he turned on his computer.

He pressed lots of keys on the keyboard, opened different windows on his screen, clicked his mouse on this and on that. Suddenly a picture appeared on the screen. And then another. And another. His cameras were all working. He could see everywhere downstairs!

Over the next few days, Ricky often stayed in his room. He was like a scientist studying his family, or a spy. He watched Sonia (her hair was dark again), he watched Jade, he followed his father, he examined his mother. He could see and hear everything they did. There was only one problem. Now his family weren't very interesting! Nothing ever happened!

At school, his friends asked:
'Hey, Ricky, can you help me with my homework tonight?'
'Can you help me with this maths problem?'
'Could you come round• and check my printer?'
But Ricky's answer was always the same.
'I'm sorry, but I can't. I'm really busy at the moment.'

Zadie and Grace watched Ricky walking away across the playground.
'What's up• with him?' asked Grace.
'I don't know,' Zadie replied. 'He's acting so weirdly•.'
'Do you think he's got a girlfriend?'
'Ricky? He only loves computers!' said Zadie, laughing.
'That's true,' said Grace. 'But maybe he's going out with• a pretty new laptop! **Ha! ha! ha!**'

Ricky was acting strangely in class, too.

Ms Cooke, the maths teacher, said, 'OK everybody. Could you give me your homework, please?'
Ricky's friends gloomily• gave her their exercise books. They knew their homework was full of wrong answers because they didn't have Ricky's help.
'Ricky? Can I have your homework, please?' asked Ms Cooke nicely. She was always nice to Ricky. He was her star student.
Ricky went red.
'Ricky? Have you got a problem?' she asked.
'Erm, I'm sorry, Ms Cooke. But... but...'
'But what?'
'I forgot to do it.'
'Are you all right?' she asked. 'Do you feel sick? You look a bit hot. Have you got a temperature?'
He touched his head.
'Er, possibly,' he said. 'But I can do the homework for tomorrow morning.'
'All right. Make sure you do,' said Ms Cooke.
And all Ricky's friends smiled.

After dinner, Ricky went up to his room, shut the door and turned on his computer. He could see his parents on the monitor, sitting at the table.

'Ricky's working much too hard,' said his mother. 'He has too much homework.'

'Don't worry about Ricky,' said his father. 'He's a very clever boy. You know, he can do the crossword in under five minutes!'

Ricky pressed a key. Now he was looking in the sitting room. Sonia was lying on the sofa sending text messages. Jade was watching TV. It was all so boring!

It didn't get any more interesting all evening. In fact, it got worse. It seemed that his great plan was a complete waste• of time and money. He had to do something. He had to make his film more exciting. And then, he had another idea.

The next morning.
6
Have you seen my mobile?
No, I haven't.
Are you sure?
Of course I'm sure.

You always use mine.
I don't have it, OK? You should take more care of your things.

Can you hear that? It's my ring tone. My mobile's somewhere in the kitchen!
bling bling bling bling

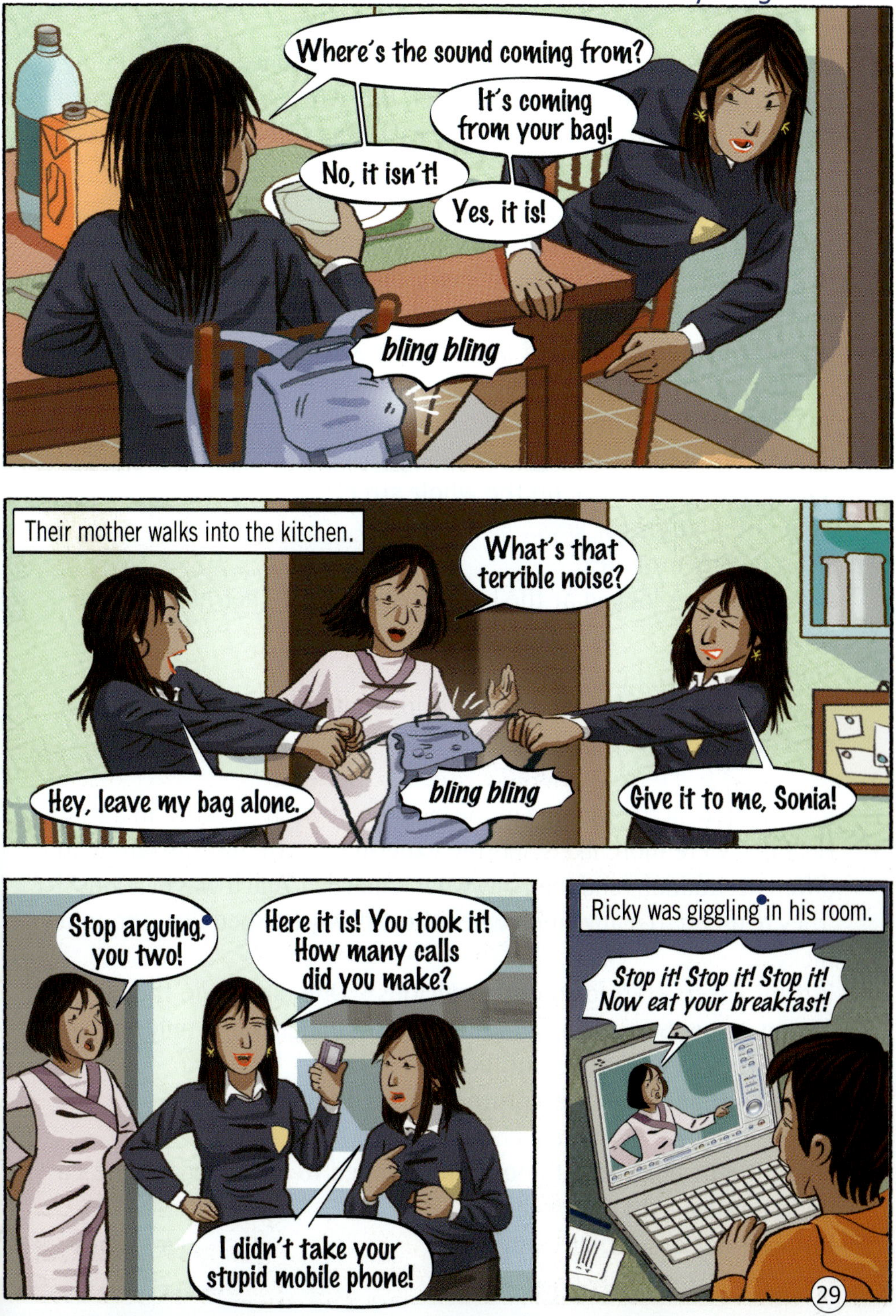
Where's the sound coming from?
It's coming from your bag!
No, it isn't!
Yes, it is!
bling bling
Their mother walks into the kitchen.
What's that terrible noise?
Hey, leave my bag alone.
bling bling
Give it to me, Sonia!
Stop arguing, you two!
Here it is! You took it! How many calls did you make?
I didn't take your stupid mobile phone!
Ricky was giggling in his room.
Stop it! Stop it! Stop it! Now eat your breakfast!

7 Over the next few days, more strange things happened in Ricky's home. Ricky's grandparents came to dinner. But when his mother opened the oven to take out the cake, the cake was still a cold wet mess•. The oven wasn't on!

Then his father lost his car keys. He couldn't find them anywhere. He searched in every room, in every drawer, down the back of the sofa and even in the fridge! He went to bed worried and annoyed•. He woke up early and went down to the kitchen... and he found his car keys on the table.
'Ayesha! AYESHA!' he shouted.
Ricky's mother hurried downstairs.
'What is it? You'll wake up the whole street!'
He pointed at his car keys.
'Who put them there?'
Ricky's mother looked at the keys, then looked at her husband.
'You did.'
'I didn't!'
'You're growing old, Jamal,' she said, smiling. 'You're losing your memory!'

Ricky edited all the footage in the evening. It wasn't 'reality' in a way. His films were more like scientific experiments. He put his family in different situations and then saw what happened. And it was hilarious•!
'They're going to really laugh when they see my finished film,' thought Ricky.
But his sisters started to get suspicious•. One day while they were having dinner, Sonia said, 'Why do all these strange things only happen to us? They never happen to Ricky.'
Sonia and Jade gave their brother an accusing look.
Ricky shrugged• and ate a chip.
His mother said, 'These things don't happen to Ricky because he's a good boy. Isn't that right, Jamal?'
But even Ricky's father wasn't sure.

It was time to stop.

So one night, Ricky went downstairs and collected all his cameras and hid them again in the bottom of his wardrobe.

And life in Ricky's home returned to normal.

But Ricky was ambitious. He didn't want to stop making films. In fact, he wanted to make bigger, better and funnier ones.

Days passed. Ricky was quiet and thoughtful. He helped his friends with their homework. He was Ms Cooke's best student again.

But Ricky was thinking. Thinking and waiting. And finally he knew what to do next.

On Monday afternoon the bell rang. School was over• for the day! Everybody got up from their desks and rushed• to the door. David was still putting his books in his bag when Ricky said, 'David, did you see this?'
Ricky was holding a message written on a piece of note paper.
'I just found it under your desk. It's for you.'
David took the piece of paper and read it quickly.

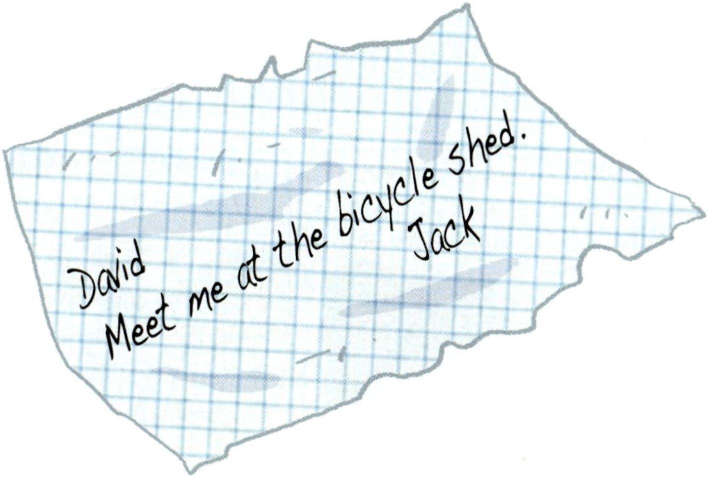

'Why did Jack write this?' asked David. 'He was here in the class five minutes ago.'
Ricky shrugged.
'Jack's a bit of a lunatic•, isn't he?'
On his way out of the classroom, David threw the note in the bin. Then he went to meet Jack.

Jack wasn't happy.
What's up, Jack?
What are you doing here?
You told me to come.
No, I didn't.
You wrote me a message.
I didn't write you a message. Where is it? Show it to me.
I threw it away.
Why are you so angry?
Why do you think? Just look at my bike.
Do you know why my tyres are flat?
Of course I don't.

Is this your idea of a joke? You don't even have a bike. Did you come here to have a laugh?
This has got nothing to do with me. I came here because you asked me to.
You're a liar, David. Come here.
I'm going home.
I said come here!
David started running. And Jack followed.
You're not going to get away with this!

9 Later that evening, Ricky was watching his monitor. He could see David and Jack running away. Then the image moved around and Ricky's face filled the screen. And he was smiling!

Ricky was smiling in real life, too. It was his best footage so far. He wanted to make an edited film as quickly as he could. So he went downstairs, said goodnight to his parents and went back to his room. But he didn't go to bed.
He worked secretly and in silence.
Later he heard someone go to the bathroom.
Then he heard voices in the road, shouting.
And all the time he was watching, cutting, adding music – making his film sharper• and funnier.
Then he heard a single bird singing in the garden. He went to the window and looked out. Grey light was in the sky. The sun was rising.
He rubbed his red eyes•. He had to get some sleep.
Two hours later there was a loud knocking at his door.
'Ricky, are you up?' his mother called out.
'Your breakfast is on the table!'

On Wednesday after school, Holly was walking home with a big pile• of library books. She had to do a project and the information she needed wasn't on the Internet. She had to use books and they were heavy!

'Can I help you with those books?' asked David.

'What?' said Holly. She didn't look friendly.

'I said can I help you with...'

'I heard what you said!'

'What is it? I was just being polite.'

'Well, I don't want you to be polite and I don't want your help. And stop looking at me like that.'

'Like what?'

'Like that! In that weird way!'

'Take it easy, Holly!' said David. She was really angry with him now and he didn't know why.

'OK, I can take it easy. But stop sending me all those stupid letters!'
David was completely confused now.
'I don't know what you're talking about.'
'I'm talking about these!'
Holly put down the library books and took a bunch of• letters from her school bag. She held them up in front of his face.
'Do you remember them now?'
David took the letters and started reading. They all started ***'My deerest• Holly'***. And they all finished with '***I love you!***'
'I didn't write these,' said David. 'And anyway, there are spelling mistakes in them. And I'm good at spelling.'
Holly thought about that for a moment. It was true. In fact, David was a brilliant writer. He was probably the best speller in the whole of Westbourne.
'Well, if you didn't write them,' said Holly, 'who did?'
David shook his head.

On Thursday afternoon, a boy was sitting in the shadows• outside a garage. He clearly didn't want anybody to see him. He was holding a laptop and studying its screen.

Inside the garage, Zadie, Grace and Holly were getting ready to start their rehearsal•. They always rehearsed in the garage of Grace's parents. That's why they called their band 'The Garage Girls'!

Zadie sat down behind her drums. Holly picked up her guitar and plugged it in• the amplifier. Grace picked up her guitar and stood in front of the microphone.

'What are we going to play?' asked Zadie.
'Let's try our new song,' said Grace. 'OK?'
'OK!' said Holly and Zadie together.

One, two, three!
THWACKTHWACKTHWACK!
KRAAANNNGGGG!
SPRAAANNNGGG!
KRANG
SPRANG
THWACKTHWACKTHWACK!
Hey, what happened to the power?
The amplifiers went dead.
What do you think, Holly?
Well, the power seems to be back again.
KRAAANNNGGGG!

OK, let's try again. Are you ready?
Let's play really loud!
Yes, I am!
But when Grace started singing, the power went again!
We are The Garage...
KRANG
SPRANG
What's going on?
Outside, Ricky was controlling the power. The girls looked so funny!
I just don't get it. Every time I start singing, the power goes.
But a wasp wasn't as amused as Ricky.
Ouch!

11 Grace, Holly and Zadie looked at each other.

'Did you hear that?' asked Grace.

'What was it?' asked Holly.

'It sounded like a shout,' said Zadie. 'There's somebody outside!'

'Who?' asked Grace.

'Come on,' said Holly. 'Let's go and find out.'

Holly pushed up the garage door, and the girls rushed out into the sunshine. They looked all around.

'Who's there?' Holly called out.

'Can you see anybody?' asked Zadie.

Grace shook her head.

'Hang on•,' said Holly. 'Look down the road.'

They saw a boy running away as fast as he could. Under his arm he was holding a laptop. They watched him disappear around the corner.

Holly scratched• her head.

''I don't know about you,' she said, 'but I think I recognised him.'

David was reading a detective novel when he got a call• on his mobile.

'Hi David.'

'Hi, Holly. What is it?'

'You know that thing about the letters...'

'Are you still getting them?' he asked.

'No, no. But something happened yesterday afternoon.'

Then Holly told David all about the rehearsal.

'And then,' continued Holly, 'I saw Sonia on my way home.'

'Sonia?'

'You know, Ricky's sister,' said Holly.

'Oh right. And?'

'Well, we started chatting and she told me about these strange things that happened in her house.'

'What kind of strange things?'

'Missing car keys. Missing mobile phones. Odd• messages. Things like that.'

'So we know who wrote those letters,' said David.

'And who did all the other stuff•,' said Holly.

'We have to stop him.'

On Friday morning, David, Holly, Grace, Zadie and Jack were standing outside the school gates. There was only one topic of conversation: Ricky.

'I knew Jack's message was odd,' said David.

'Yeah,' said Jack. 'The message said "bicycle shed•". I never say "bicycle". I always say "bike". '

'Then I received a letter from David every day,' said Holly.

'They were full of spelling mistakes!' said David.

'David never makes spelling mistakes!'

'Then we found a camera in my parents' garage,' said Grace.

'What kind of camera?' asked Jack.

'It was a little video camera,' explained Zadie.

'A video camera? Wow,' said Jack. 'Do you think he was filming you?'

'Yes, I do,' said Zadie.

'But why?' asked Jack.

'Don't you remember that video Ricky showed us?' asked David. 'You know, the one about his sister and her blue hair.'

'Oh yeah, that's right!' said Jack. 'He really thought his film was funny.'

'I bet• he was filming us in the garage, too,' said Zadie. 'And he was filming you and David. And David and Holly.'

'He was filming all of us?' asked Jack.

'That's right,' she said. 'So he could make his silly films.'

'Sssh, stop talking,' said Grace. 'Here he comes.'

Ricky was walking towards them on the pavement. He had dark rings• around his eyes. He looked very tired.

'Hi, Ricky,' said David.

'Oh, hi,' said Ricky. But Ricky didn't stop to chat. He carried on walking across the playground and into the school.

Ricky had another bad day. He couldn't remember dates in history, he forgot the symbols for chemicals in science, and he got the wrong answers in maths.

When school was over, Ricky crossed the playground again and walked out of the gates. But he didn't get any further. His friends were waiting for him. And they had lots of questions.

'What are you doing, Ricky?'

'Why are you filming us?'

'What are you going to do with your films?'

'Why are you playing games• with us?'

'Have you got the films with you?'

'Can we see them?'

To the last two questions, Ricky said 'yes'.

'OK,' said Holly, 'let's watch them now. Ricky, you're coming home with us.'

And with Ricky in the middle, they all walked back to Holly's house.

An hour later, they were all sitting in Holly's sitting room. The films were over. They all agreed they were very well made. In fact, they were brilliant. But the friends weren't happy.

'What do you plan to do with them?' asked Holly.

'I'm going to put them on my website,' said Ricky.

'You can't do that,' said Grace.

'But they're really funny!' said Ricky. 'And I worked so hard on them!'

'I think the film about your sisters is funny,' said Jack. 'And the one about your parents. But not the one with me.'

'And not the one with me,' said David.

'Or the one with me,' said Holly.

'Or me,' said Zadie.

'Or me,' added Grace.

'No way•,' said Jack. 'I mean, you didn't ask our permission• or anything.'

'You tried to make us look silly,' said Grace.

'And you made us angry with each other,' said Holly.

'You just don't do that to your friends,' said David.

That night, Ricky couldn't sleep. He was tired, unbelievably tired, but sleep was impossible. He lay on his bed and stared• at the ceiling. And when he wasn't staring at the ceiling, he looked at his clock. Its bright numbers were shining in the dark.

It wasn't fair. Everybody was annoyed with him. They said he was a bad friend. But they also said his films were fantastic. They all said that. And they were right. His films were good. Really good. And he had big ambitions. These short films were only the beginning. He wanted to make bigger, better, more expensive films. He wanted to go to Hollywood. But to go to Hollywood, he had to show his films. He had to put them online for the whole world to see. He only had to turn on his computer and click the mouse.

Ricky looked at the clock.

This was terrible. He was so tired but he was so wide awake• at the same time! And while he was lying on his bed, his brain was working fast. His mind was like a film. He couldn't control it. Images came and went, one after the other.

He saw himself in Hollywood.

He was on a TV. A smiling man in a fancy suit• was interviewing him. And David was wearing a fancy suit, too.

'I just love your movies•, Ricky,' he said. 'We all love your movies here in Hollywood.'

And then the audience started clapping•. Somebody cheered•. A woman shouted 'Yeah!' And then the whole audience was standing and cheering and waving and applauding. The audience were calling out to him.

'We love you, Ricky!'

'You're the greatest director in the world!'

'You're the best ever!'

The audience rushed onto the stage and picked him up. They placed him on their shoulders and carried him out of the studio into the Californian sun. A crowd was waiting for him. They all started cheering and throwing flowers at him. He saw big banners with 'RICKY THE NEW KING OF HOLLYWOOD' on them. And he saw...

He saw his family and friends. They were in a small group at the back of the crowd. They weren't waving or smiling. They were looking at him in silence. And then they turned and walked away until just Holly and David were left.

Ricky sat up in bed. He felt hot and cold and sick all at the same time.

He got up and turned on his computer.

It was a typical English summer morning. The sky was grey and the air was cool. It wasn't like Hollywood.

Ricky was walking slowly to school with David. Ricky was talking and David was listening. Sometimes he nodded•.

When they got to school, the rest of his friends were chatting in the playground. Ricky and David walked over to join them.

'Hi.'

'Hi.'

'Are you OK, Ricky?'

'I'm OK now,' said Ricky. 'And I want you to know that I deleted the films.'

'What?'

'I deleted them,' said Ricky. I can't show them to the world. They don't exist anymore. And one more thing. I'm sorry, guys. I'm really sorry.'

The friends didn't know what to say. In one way they were pleased. But in another, they were very sad for Ricky, too.

Ricky walked towards the entrance to the school.
'Wait a minute,' said David.
Ricky stopped and turned.
'I have an idea,' said David. 'A big idea.'
Ricky smiled sadly. His own big idea was a total disaster.
'Why don't you make a film?' said David.
'I made films,' said Ricky, 'and you didn't like them.'
'I mean a *real* film,' said David. 'Listen. You're a fantastic camera operator and a brilliant director. I can write the screenplay•. Grace can compose• the music. And you've got some cool• actors.'
Jack, Holly and Zadie smiled.
'We're very good-looking, too,' said Jack.
'So, what do you think, Ricky? Is that a good idea?' asked David.
'It's a very good idea, David,' said Ricky. 'Let's make a film.'

And that's exactly what happened.

David wrote an exciting screenplay about a boy with super powers. Grace composed amazing music. Zadie, Holly and Jack went to the rehearsals and learned all their lines. Well, Jack learned most of them. He wasn't very good at remembering words, but he was great at running and jumping and doing physical acting. Then Grace wanted to act in the film as well. And even David, who was very shy, became an actor, too.

Ricky planned everything. He planned the cameras, the lighting•, the costumes, the sets•. He worked for hours every evening and every weekend. And he loved every minute of it.

Three months later, everything was ready. At half past eight on a Saturday morning, Ricky spoke to his actors.
'Is everybody ready?' he asked.
'We're ready,' they said.
'OK then,' said Ricky.

After Reading

Understanding the story

1 Who says these things? Write the names beside the speech bubbles.

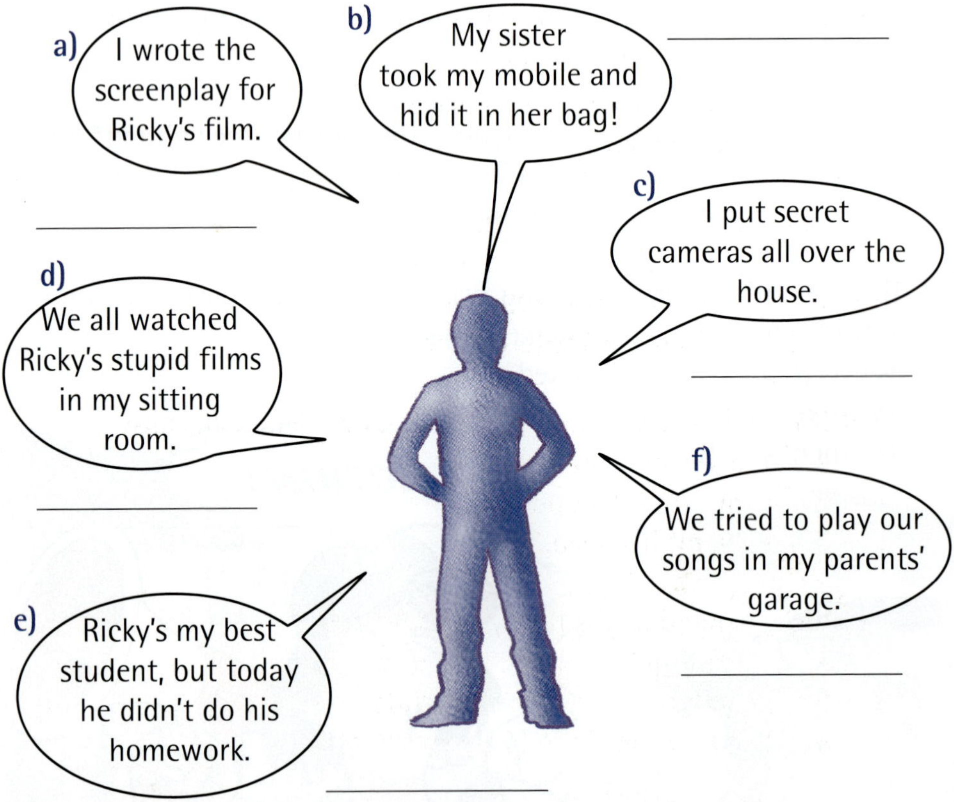

2 Now put the sentences above in the correct order of the story.

1	2	3	4	5	6

3 Complete the sentences. Tick (✓) the correct ending.

a) Ricky ran upstairs because
   1 ☐ he heard his mobile phone.
   2 ☐ he knew the answer to his maths problem.
   3 ☐ he heard his sister scream.

b) David went to see Jack in the bicycle shed because
   1 ☐ Jack wrote him a message.
   2 ☐ Ricky gave him a message.
   3 ☐ David wanted to talk to him.

c) Holly was angry with David because
   1 ☐ she thought he was sending her letters.
   2 ☐ he was in love with her.
   3 ☐ he didn't want to carry her books.

d) Ricky made a loud noise outside Holly's garage because
   1 ☐ a wasp stung him.
   2 ☐ he started laughing.
   3 ☐ he hit his head.

e) Ricky deleted all his funny films because
   1 ☐ he didn't like them anymore.
   2 ☐ he felt bad about his friends.
   3 ☐ he was going to Hollywood.

4 You are going to make a film. What kind of film do you want to make? What's it going to be about? Who are the characters going to be? Discuss your ideas with a partner.

After Reading

Vocabulary

1 Solve the anagrams then complete the sentences.

YFNUN

STEPU TUIQE

ZINGAMA STVEECLER

LBRIINTAL GREINTETINS

Ricky was the **(a)** .... boy in the school. He thought that doing maths calculations in his head was **(b)**..............................
When he saw Sonia blue hair he laughed. He thought it was very **(c)** .... Sonia didn't agree. She was very **(d)** ....
Ricky filmed Sonia, then showed the film to David and Jack. Jack loved it. He said it was **(e)** ....
After that, Ricky was very **(f)** .... at school. He was thinking hard.
But then he had a **(g)** .... idea. He could make his own reality TV programme!

2 Match the sentences with the meanings.

a) ☐ What's going on?	1	It was very annoying.
b) ☐ Take it easy.	2	I really like it.
c) ☐ It was a real pain.	3	Wait
d) ☐ I'm crazy about it.	4	I don't understand.
e) ☐ Is this your idea of a joke?	5	Relax
f) ☐ I don't get it.	6	Do you think this is funny?
g) ☐ Hang on.	7	What's happening?

3 Complete the sentences with the adverbs of manner below.

QUICKLY SLOWLY sadly HAPPILY loudly quietly ANGRILY calmly strangely sleepily

a) Ricky walked .... downstairs in the middle of the night.
b) 'Stop sending me text messages!' said Holly ....
c) Ricky looked .... at the clock. It was 03:00!
d) 'We are The Garage Girls!' Grace sang ....
e) 'I'm going to lose all my friends,' Ricky thought ....
f) 'This is the best film in the world,' said Ricky ....

4 How do they say these sentences? Choose adverbs from exercise 3.

a)

b)

c)

d)

After Reading

Grammar

Practise the Present Continuous

1 Find 12 verbs in the word square. Then write them in the Past Simple below.

T	E	W	Q	U	O	E	F	G	H
B	I	O	A	R	T	A	B	R	E
U	P	D	E	R	S	T	A	N	D
Y	T	U	R	U	I	A	V	O	O
T	Z	X	K	N	O	W	O	E	N
H	G	E	S	H	I	R	T	B	S
C	O	F	F	Y	C	I	H	I	E
O	D	S	A	M	E	T	A	K	E
M	M	A	K	E	H	E	A	R	D
E	A	Y	R	I	B	G	R	A	D

2 Now use some of the verbs to complete the sentences.

a) When Ricky .... Sonia's hair he started laughing.
b) Ricky .... lots of cameras and things from his favourite shop.
c) 'Ricky's acting so weirdly at the moment,' .... Grace.
d) Ayesha .... the cake out of the oven and saw a horrible mess.
e) David .... the screenplay for Ricky's film.

3 **Complete the sentences with verbs in brackets. Use the Past Simple or the Past Continuous.**

a) While Einstein .... (look) in a mirror he .... (have) a great idea.
b) Ricky .... (lie) on the sofa when he .... (hear) a terrible scream.
c) Sonia's parents .... (eat) breakfast when they .... (see) her hair.
d) Ricky .... (show) David a message while he .... (pack) his bag.
e) While The Garage Girls .... (play) a song, the power .... (stop).
f) Ricky .... (walk) to school when he .... (meet) his friends.

Practise questions

4 **Complete the interview with Ricky. Use the correct tenses.**

Interviewer: Hello, Ricky, and welcome to the show.
Ricky: It's great to be here.
Interviewer: When .... ?
Ricky: I started making movies six months ago.
Interviewer: What .... ?
Ricky: I was going to school at Westbourne High.
Interviewer: .... ?
Ricky: Yes, I was. I was a very good student.
Interviewer: What .... ?
Ricky: My friends didn't like my films.
Interviewer: .... ?
Ricky: I'm going to make a film here in the United States!
Interviewer: Well, you're a great director, Ricky. Good luck with the new film!
Ricky: Thank you.

After Reading

Test

1 Listen and tick (✓) the correct picture.

a) 1 ☐

2 ☐

3 ☐

b) 1 ☐

2 ☐

3 ☐

c) 1 ☐

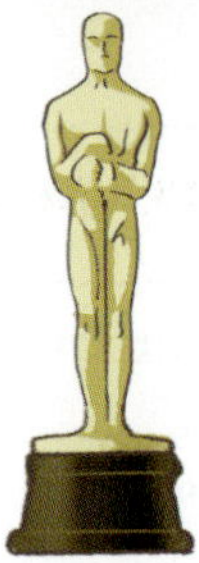

2 ☐

3 ☐

d) 1 ☐

2 ☐

3 ☐

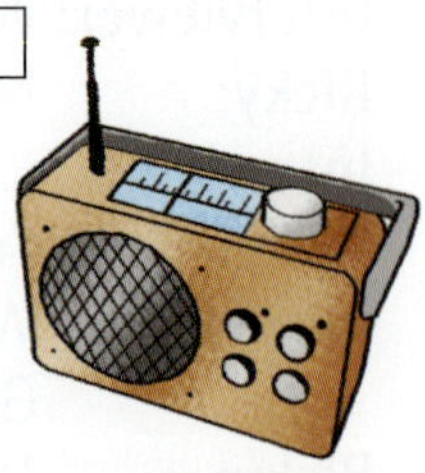

2 Read the sentences about the story and choose the best word (1, 2 or 3) for each space.

a) Ricky is good at doing maths calculations in his ....
1 notebook 2 head 3 free time

b) Ricky stops filming his family when they become ....
1 1suspicious 2 boring 3 tired

c) Jack is angry because his bicycle has two flat ....
1 seats 2 handles 3 tyres

d) When Holly sees the boy running away, she thinks that she .... him.
1 hears 2 recognises 3 shouts at

e) Ricky dreams he is on a chat show in ....
1 London 2 New York 3 Hollywood

f) Ricky finds out that he likes making real ....
1 films 2 friends 3 TV programmes

3 Look at the picture on pages 52 and 53 of the story. Ask and answer questions about it.

- Who can you see in the picture?
- What is Ricky doing?

Glossary

11 **Eureka:** I found it (it = the answer)
float: stay on the surface of water
poured: flowed out of the bath
sink: go under the surface of water
12 **gravity:** the force that pulls objects towards the centre of the earth
13 **beam:** a straight line (of light or laser)
14 **checked:** controlled; looked at the results
got them right: got the correct result
in his head: in his mind or brain
scream: loud shout
16 **dye:** colour for hair
19 **crossword:** a grid where you fit words by solving clues.
somehow: for a reason that you can't explain
20 **amazing:** incredible
didn't have enough footage: didn't film all of the scene
edited: included or excluded parts of a scene
mind: be worried; be concerned
21 **look:** expression
pain: annoying thing
the right footage: the right scene
22 **advice:** information and help
crazy about: enthusiastic about
hid it: put it away secretly
savings: money saved
23 **crept:** walked quietly
snoring: making a loud breathing noise when asleep
thief: person stealing other people's property
24 **landing:** area at the top of stairs between the bedrooms
25 **come round:** come to my house
going out with: seeing a girlfriend; dating
weirdly: in a strange way
what's up...?: what's the problem...?
26 **gloomily:** sadly, unhappily
27 **waste:** bad use

29 **arguing:** being angry with each other
giggling: laughing in a quiet way
30 **annoyed:** cross; angry
hilarious: very funny
shrugged: lifted his shoulders to say 'I don't know'
suspicious: feeling that something is wrong
wet mess: watery mixture
33 **lunatic:** person who does crazy things
over: finished
rushed: went quickly
35 **liar:** person who tells lies
36 **rubbed his red eyes:** moved his hands over his eyes
sharper: more precise
37 **pile:** one on top of the other
38 **bunch of:** large amount of
deerest: wrong spelling of 'dearest'
39 **plugged it in:** connected it to
rehearsal: practice time for a performance
shadows: darkness
40 **dead:** not working
power: electricity
42 **hang on:** wait
scratched: rubbed with her hands
43 **call:** phone call
odd: strange
stuff: things
44 **bet:** think; imagine
rings: circles
shed: small building, usually of wood, to keep things in
46 **playing games:** playing tricks
47 **no way:** absolutely not
permission: when you say someone can do something
48 **stared:** looked fixedly
49 **cheered:** shouted to express support
clapping: applauding
fancy suit: expensive trousers and jacket
movies: films (in American English)
wide awake: completely conscious, with his eyes fully open

51 **nodded:** moved his head up and down to say 'yes'
52 **compose:** write music
operator: user; person who makes something work
screenplay: the words of a film
53 **lighting:** lights used to achieve a particular effect
sets: scenery